STAR WARS™

MEET THE GALACTIC HEROES

T0015024

Disney • LUCASFILM PRESS

Los Angeles • New York

CONTENTS

STAR WARS

THIS IS OBI-WAN

WRITTEN BY EMELI JUHLIN
ART BY TITMOUSE AND TOMATOFARM

This is Obi-Wan Kenobi.
Obi-Wan is a Jedi Master.

Jedi protect peace and justice
in the galaxy.

Before he was a Jedi Master,
Obi-Wan was a Padawan.
He was trained
by Qui-Gon Jinn.

Qui-Gon meets Anakin.
He wants Anakin to train
to become a Jedi Knight.

The evil Darth Maul
defeats Qui-Gon.
Obi-Wan fights Darth Maul.

Obi-Wan will train Anakin
in the ways of the Force.
The Force is a magic energy field
that connects all living things.

Obi-Wan goes on a mission
for the Republic to Kamino.

He finds an army
made of clones.
Clones are copies
of a person.

Obi-Wan meets Jango
and Boba Fett.
Jango is a bounty hunter.
The clones are copies of him.

Obi-Wan tries to take Jango
to the Jedi Council
for questioning.

Jango attacks Obi-Wan.

Obi-Wan must defend himself!

He uses his lightsaber.

A lighstaber is a laser sword.
Obi-Wan cannot stop Jango.
Jango escapes!

Obi-Wan follows Jango
to a secret meeting.
The sinister Count Dooku
plans to take control
of the Republic.

Count Dooku starts a war.
Obi-Wan leads the clones
into battle.

Obi-Wan and Anakin
fight Count Dooku.

Anakin turns to the dark side.
Obi-Wan must stop him.

All Anakin wants is power.

Anakin becomes Darth Vader.
He serves the evil
Emperor Palpatine.

Obi-Wan fights Darth Vader.

He knows he has lost his friend
to the dark side forever.

Obi-Wan grows old.

A droid named R2-D2 visits him.

R2-D2 has a message.

Princess Leia needs help

to stop Darth Vader.

Obi-Wan wants Luke Skywalker
to come with him
to help Princess Leia.

Obi-Wan and Luke
meet Han Solo and Chewbacca.
They pilot the *Millennium Falcon*.

Luke and Obi-Wan
must stay hidden.
Darth Vader cannot know
where they are.

Darth Vader finds out
where they are.
They must escape!

Obi-Wan teaches Luke
to use the Force.

Darth Vader captures
the *Millennium Falcon*.
They are trapped
on the Death Star.

Obi-Wan must fight Vader
one last time.
Luke and the others escape
from the Death Star.

Obi-Wan becomes one
with the Force.
He will always be there
for the people who need him.

STAR WARS™

THIS IS LEIA

WRITTEN BY EMELI JUHLIN

ART BY TITMOUSE AND TOMATOFARM

This is Leia Organa.

Leia is a princess.

She is from Alderaan.

Alderaan is a peaceful planet.
Leia loves to explore it
with her droid, Lola.

Leia meets Obi-Wan Kenobi.
Obi-Wan is a Jedi.
They become friends.

Obi-Wan gives Leia a holster.
It once belonged
to a great leader.
Leia will be
a great leader.

When she grows up,
Leia sends a message
to Obi-Wan.
She needs his help.

Darth Vader captures
Princess Leia.
He will destroy Alderaan
if she tries to stop him.

With help from her new friends,
Leia escapes Vader!

Leia goes to Cloud City with
Chewie, R2-D2, Luke, Han,
and C-3PO.

In Cloud City,
Han's friend Lando
promises to help them.

It's a trick!
Darth Vader is waiting
for them.

Han is taken.

Lando feels bad.

He helps Leia and

the others escape.

Leia flies the *Millennium Falcon* away from Cloud City.

Leia dresses up
like a bounty hunter.
She rescues Han
from Jabba the Hutt.

Leia and her friends go to
the Forest Moon of Endor.

They need to destroy
the Empire's superweapon.
It is called a Death Star.
The Death Star floats
above Endor.

Leia meets an Ewok
named Wicket.
Leia wants to save Wicket's home.

Leia, Han, and Chewie
fight stormtroopers.
Wicket and the other
Ewoks fight, too.

Lando pilots the *Falcon*.
He helps the rebel ships
destroy the Death Star!

Thanks to Leia and her friends, the Ewoks' home and the galaxy are saved.

Years later, Leia becomes a general.
She must stop the First Order.
They have a new superweapon.

It is called the Starkiller.
General Leia sends a pilot
named Poe Dameron
to destroy the Starkiller.

The mission is a success,
but the Resistance
is still in danger.

The First Order finds out
where the Resistance is hiding.
They come to attack.

Leia calls for help.

The Resistance is trapped.
Leia and the rebels
try to find a way out.

A Jedi named Rey helps them.
They still have hope.

Leia becomes Rey's Jedi Master.
Leia trains Rey in the ways
of the Force.

Leia is a princess
and a general.

She is a brave leader
and a loyal friend.

Leia's legacy lives on.

STAR WARS™

THIS IS LUKE

WRITTEN BY NATE MILLICI
ART BY TOMATOFARM

This is Luke.
Luke lives on a
sandy planet.

But Luke is bored.
Luke wants to leave
the sandy planet.

Luke meets two droids.

The tall one is C-3PO.

The short one is R2-D2.

They have a secret message.

R2-D2 shows Luke
the secret message.
It is from Princess Leia.
She needs help.

Luke wants to help the princess.

He meets Obi-Wan.

Obi-Wan is a Jedi Knight.

He will train Luke.

Jedi Knights use the Force.

The Force is a magic energy field.

Jedi Knights use a special sword.

It is called a lightsaber.

Luke leaves the sandy planet.

He finds Princess Leia.

She is trapped on the Death Star.

Luke and Leia escape!

The Death Star is a
space station.
It can destroy planets.
Luke and R2-D2
must stop the Death Star.

Luke flies his X-wing fighter.
Luke uses the Force.
He destroys the Death Star!

Luke travels to a snowy planet.
A snow monster traps Luke.
Luke uses the Force
to reach his lightsaber.

Luke uses his lightsaber.
He stops the snow monster!

Giant AT-AT walkers stomp
across the snowy planet.
Luke uses his lightsaber to
stop them, too!

Luke goes to a swamp planet
to find Yoda.
Yoda is a Jedi Master.
Yoda is strong in the Force.

Yoda is a good teacher.
And Luke is a good student.
Yoda teaches Luke how to
be a Jedi Knight.

Princess Leia, C-3PO, and Chewie
are in trouble.
Luke leaves the swamp planet.
He must help his friends!

Luke fights Darth Vader.
Darth Vader was a great
Jedi Knight.
But he turned to the dark side.

Now Darth Vader is evil.
He wants Luke
to join the dark side.
Luke does not want
to join the dark side.

Luke faces more villains.
He escapes from
Jabba the Hutt.

He fights Boba Fett.

Luke also makes new friends.
He travels to a forest moon.
He meets the Ewoks.

Ewoks are small and furry.
They help Luke and his friends.

Luke meets Darth Vader again.
Luke is trapped!

Darth Vader takes Luke
to the evil Emperor.
He wants Luke to join
the dark side, too.

Luke fights Darth Vader
for the last time.

Luke does not give in
to fear or anger.
He will never join the dark side!

Luke is not bored anymore.

He is a brave hero.

Luke is a great Jedi Knight!

THIS IS REY

WRITTEN BY EMELI JUHLIN

ART BY TITMOUSE AND TOMATOFARM

This is Rey.
Rey lives on
a sandy planet.

She is alone.
She wants to find
her family.

Rey sells parts of
old ships for food.

Rey saves a small droid
from a sand dweller.
The droid's name is BB-8.

Rey will not sell BB-8
even though she is hungry.

Rey and BB-8 meet Finn.
Finn ran away
from the evil First Order.

The First Order is also
looking for BB-8.
They run to an old ship.

Rey flies the old ship
called the *Millennium Falcon*.
The First Order chases them.

Finn and Rey make a good team.
They escape the First Order.
They find the Resistance.

General Leia sends Rey
on a mission to find
Luke Skywalker.

Rey asks for Luke's help.
She tries to give him
his old lightsaber.

A lightsaber is a laser sword.

Luke does not want it.

He does not want to fight.

Rey will not leave
without Luke.

Luke agrees to teach Rey
about the Force.
The Force is an energy field.

She practices with
Luke's lightsaber.
She loses control.

Luke is afraid of Rey's power.
He won't go with her
to stop the First Order.

Rey knows General Leia
and her friends need her.
She leaves Luke behind.

The First Order TIE fighters
attack the rebel base.
Rey flies the *Millennium Falcon*
and blasts the TIE fighters.

Rey looks for her friends.

Rey finds a pile of rocks
trapping her friends.
She uses the Force
to move the rocks.

General Leia thanks Rey
for her help.

Kylo Ren is the Supreme Leader
of the First Order.
He is connected to Rey
through the Force.

Rey wants Kylo to
turn to the light side.
Kylo wants Rey to
turn to the dark side.

Rey learns that her grandfather is the evil Emperor Palpatine. Luke visits Rey through the Force. He knows Rey is afraid of her power.

She must face her fear
like a true Jedi.
Luke gives her Leia's lightsaber.

Luke gives her his
old X-wing starship.
Rey has what she needs.
She must face her grandfather.

Emperor Palpatine wants Rey
to take his throne.
Rey does not want
to lead the First Order.

Kylo Ren turns to the light side.

His real name is Ben.

Rey and Ben face
the Emperor together.

Rey stops the Emperor's
Force lightning.

She destroys him
once and for all.

Luke and Leia are her family now.
She becomes a Skywalker.
Rey is a Jedi!

STAR WARS™

THESE ARE THE DROIDS

WRITTEN BY EMELI JUHLIN

ART BY TITMOUSE AND TOMATOFARM

These are the droids
you are looking for.

R2-D2, C-3PO, and BB-8
have been on many missions.

Anakin Skywalker built C-3PO
to help his mother.
C-3PO meets R2-D2
on a sandy planet.

C-3PO is tall.

He is very serious.

R2-D2 is short.

He is very helpful.

Years later, R2-D2 and C-3PO
go back to the sandy planet.
They get lost.
They are captured by Jawas!

Luke Skywalker rescues the droids.
They meet Obi-Wan Kenobi.
Obi-Wan is a Jedi.

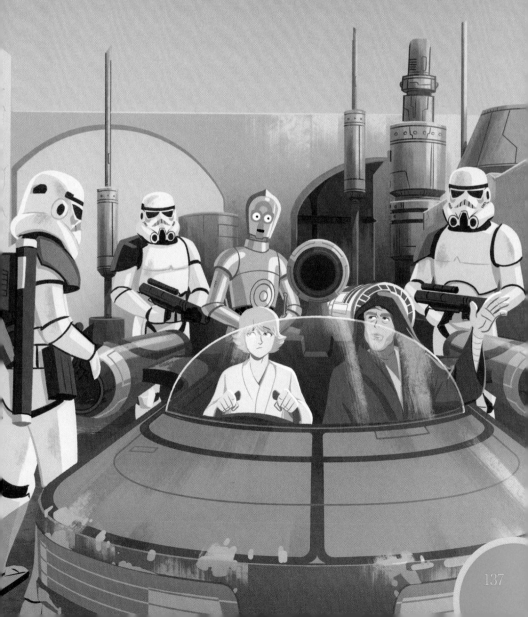

R2-D2 and C-3PO go with
Luke and Obi-Wan
on their mission
to help Princess Leia.

R2-D2 and C-3PO help save Leia.

Luke has to destroy
the Death Star.
It is a superweapon.
R2-D2 flies with Luke.

Later, on an icy planet,
the rebels are in trouble.
The evil Darth Vader
has found their base.

C-3PO escapes with Leia,
Chewie, and Han.

R2-D2 stays behind with Luke.

R2-D2 is a loyal droid.

He goes wherever help is needed.

R2-D2 and Luke go to
a swamp planet.
Luke trains with Jedi
Master Yoda.
Luke becomes a Jedi.

Years later, Luke does not want
to be a Jedi anymore.
He goes into hiding.
BB-8 has a map to find Luke.

BB-8 is short and round.

He is very playful.

BB-8 meets Rey.

The First Order wants the map.

BB-8 must protect the map.

Rey protects BB-8.

Rey and BB-8 meet Finn.
Finn is also hiding from
the First Order.
They all escape.

BB-8 meets C-3PO and R2-D2.

BB-8 gives the map
to the Resistance.
They need Luke's help.

First BB-8 and a pilot
named Poe go on a mission.
They must destroy the Starkiller.

The Starkiller is a weapon made by the First Order. The Starkiller is destroyed!

Then R2-D2 finds Luke.
He plays an old message from Leia.
It reminds Luke of his past.
He will help.

Even with Luke's help,
the Resistance needs information.
The First Order is hiding secrets.
BB-8 must find them.

BB-8 finds the secrets.
The Resistance now has
their first clue.

When they find all the clues,
they will know how to stop
the First Order!

They find a new clue.
They are one step closer
to stopping the First Order.

The heroes continue
their adventures.

These droids will do anything
to help their friends
and save the galaxy!